Ashley is a new author, hoping to create books her niece and nephew can grow up reading. Being from the North East of England she has grown up a Newcastle United fan and is also a supporter of women's football. She is very family orientated and when she is not working enjoys time at home or weekend trips away.

THE BIG DREAM

ASHLEY RADWELL

AUSTIN MACAULEY PUBLISHERS™
LONDON ★ CAMBRIDGE ★ NEW YORK ★ SHARJAH

A CIP catalogue record for this title is available from the British Library.

ISBN 9781398465213 (Paperback)
ISBN 9781398473621 (ePub-e-book)

www.austinmacauley.com

First Published 2024
Austin Macauley Publishers Ltd˙
1 Canada Square
Canary Wharf
London
E14 5AA

Thank you to Austin Macauley Publishers for being patient with me and assisting with each stage of the process.

To Cheryl - thank you for encouraging me to start this book.

For my family who constantly support me, and for Olivia and Lewis who have inspired me to write.

For the Lionesses for inspiring a generation and for giving me one of the best moments of my life!

Alex is like any other pupil at Bluedale High School, filled with a mix of nerves and excitement about starting a new school year. At 13 years old, starting a new year wasn't unexpected for Alex, but this year was different. Year 9 was allowed to try out for the school football team! Alex's mum made the traditional 'first day breakfast' (which Alex pretended to hate but secretly loved) for her and her little brother, George; a giant stack of pancakes with bananas and syrup. After breakfast, Alex's dad drove her and George to school, dropping George first at the middle school around the corner and then off to Bluedale High for Alex's first day of Year 9.

At 9am, the familiar sound of the bell ringing signalled the beginning of assembly. The entire school year gathered into the Main Hall where the head of year welcomed back the students from the summer break. After assembly, Alex and a couple of her friends went to collect their timetable and they all gathered in a huddle to compare who had the best teachers and how many classes they shared. Alex immediately checked when her first PE lesson was; this would be her first opportunity to check with the teachers the date and time of the football trials.

After the first day, nerves were out of the way. Bluedale high settled down for the students to embed themselves into a new term. One of her first lessons was English, where Mrs Hampton asked the pupils to note down some aims and objectives, both academically and personally that they wanted to achieve by the end of the year. Alex struggled with this as the only objective firmly at the top of her priority list was getting onto the football team. Since being very young, Alex can remember her dad taking her down to the park to join in with the older kids for a game of five a side. If her dad was honest, this was just to keep Alex and her never ending energy levels busy and focused on something that was keeping her both healthy and socialising with other kids. Through playing football with the older kids around the village, Alex had noticed that she already knew quite a few boys and girls in the years above. This definitely helped when she had to ask John, who usually plays in goal for them where her science lab was. Alex couldn't wait until her first lesson and went early to see one of the PE teachers to check when football trials were. Thankfully she didn't have to wait too long as her year group were trying out on Tuesday – the next night.

Finally after what felt like the longest night of her life, Tuesday had arrived and it was time for PE. Alex and a group of other year 9 were all sprinting to the changing rooms to get out onto the school pitches as quickly as possible. As she was getting changed a few of the girls were talking about the various school teams they wanted to join, it was a pretty even mix between people who wanted to join Netball, cricket, tennis and football. The girls were all pointing to the posters with the different trial dates on. Alex couldn't wait for that night and was glad that she didn't have to wait until Friday for the cricket trials! Alex's first PE lesson went really well. She loved any form of sport and after watching Wimbledon every summer, Tennis was definitely a good way to start the term.

At break time, Alex texted her parents to tell them she will be about an hour late because she was going to the football trials. They both texted back wishing her good luck. Her dad also added his usual piece of advice which is usually never far from Alex's mind when she is playing, 'believe in yourself, kid'. Alex has a long list of players in the Women's Super League who she grew up idolising: Steph Houghton, VivianneMiedema, Leah Williamson and Demi Stokes, just to name a few, and since watching Change to 'Alessia Russo score that backheel against Sweden in the Semi-finals of the Euros', shehad always dreamt of recreating a moment like that. Time seamed to stand still waiting for the end of the day, wishing the lessons away so she could get back down to the training pitches. Alex bought an extra banana at lunch so she could eat that before she went down to get changed.

The bell signalled the end of the day and while most of the pupils rushed for the school exit, Alex and a couple of others from her Maths class made their way down to the changing rooms for the second time that day then the butterflies began. There were more people than Alex expected. The mix was about half boys and half girls; they were split into small groups for warm ups. After the warm ups, they practiced a few different skills, dribbling through cones, sprints, and Alex's favourite – shooting.

There was a good amount of people that the session could end with a couple of small games. This was where Alex knew the pressure was on – make an impact here and she had a chance of making it onto the team. The games were both pretty even which would only make it harder for the coaches to make their decision.

Her game was 1–0 down and it was late on in the second half, Alex had a few moments on the ball and managed to assist their first goal, passing to Adam for him to slot it into the bottom corner. In what must have been some of the last minutes in the game, Alex's team won a corner and this was going to be a battle between her and the defence for how the game would end. In came the corner and Sarah at the front post chipped it on to fall at perfect knee height for a volley from Alex, after watching the ball leave her foot she held her breath. The keeper dived for it but they had no chance – back of the net! Alex had won the game for her team! The other game finished 3–2 so Alex knew that it wasn't just her that would be competing for the striker position,but this didn't dampen her celebrations or wipe the smile off her face.

As the week went on, Alex grew more and more doubtful about her performance in the trial. Did she show enough hunger for the ball? Were the other players going to stand out more than her? Alex's parents noticed that she wasn't her usual bubbly self and tried to reassure her that everything happens for a reason and regardless of if she makes the team or not, this won't stop her love for playing the game. Sitting in geography trying to focus on Mr Bishop's messy hard to read notes, Alex heard Beth at the back of the class mumble something about the school teams. Pretending to ask for a pen, Alex asked her if she knew when they squad announcement was. Apparently, Beth had heard that the teams are being posted on the school website at 7pm tonight. And as soon as she had heard that, Alex got a knot in her stomach. Tonight she will find out either way if she has made the team.

As the family were finishing their tea (Alex had managed to eat one fish finger and then just moved some peas back and forth around her plate until she gave up and scraped her plate in the bin). Alex's dad loaded up the school website and started occasionally refreshing the page to see if the squad would be announced early. As the time agonisingly hit 7pm with no announcement, Alex moved her dad out of the way and frantically began hitting the refresh button until finally at 7:06pm a new post appeared. Alex couldn't move the mouse quick enough to navigate to the link and wait for it to open, then the list was there each member of the family were huddled around the laptop to scan over the lucky squad members. About five seconds passed then a voice from behind mum said 'YOU DID IT, ALEX' then pointed about three quarters down the screen to where her name was. The whole family cheered and leaped around as if they had just won the lottery, and for Alex it felt like she had. This is it, she thought, *this was what I need to begin my football journey with a team.*

The days could not pass quick enough to get to Monday again for the first training session for Bluedale High FC. The cones were out, the balls were there and the bibs were on. Alex was joined by a few of her friends on the team which gave her a welcomed feeling of support to go with the equal mix of excitement and pressure to perform. The coaches started the warm up with a series of stretches, explaining which muscle group this was warming up and why it was so important. Throughout the practice, Alex found herself pushing herself physically further and further until Mr Scott took her to one side and asked if she was okay. 'Yes, but I just want to impress you. I can't lose my place.' Mr Scott explained to her that as long as she wanted to be on the team then the space was hers – she had already passed the trial. Mr Scott also explained that the real intensity needs to be on the pitch when there is a game. If she was at 100% all of the time, then she will quickly burn herself out. The training session neared to an end and after they worked on marking and passing drills, they played a quick couple of matches. The coaches were rotating the substitutes regularly to both make sure everyone got some game time and also to try to begin to see the chemistry some players had and how they worked together.

Although Alex went for a kick about most nights after school, she found herself wishing the week away to get back to training on a Monday night. There was something about the structure she was given that she thrived on, every tip and piece of training advice was memorised and Alex tried to practice these as much as she could. Alex was beginning to make more friends within the team and her confidence was growing. The coach decided to finish one training session with a penalty shoot-out. Alex had actually never taken a penalty as there was always a lack of volunteers to be a referee when she played in the park and neither side could ever agree to award one. But as she was a striker, this was something that she would inevitably one day need to master. Each player lined up and the penalties began. As there were a mix of all different positions, the quality of the kicks varied, some straight to the keeper, some top corner and about a third of them straight over the bar. As the line got shorter and shorter Alex began to second guess herself, in her head she was changing the side she was going to go for. Finally she was up. She placed the ball and tried to stare straight at the keeper to see if she could fool her into thinking she was confident. Up she stepped and Alex watched as the ball went just wide of the left hand post.She couldn't believe it. A striker who can't score a penalty. *'What good am I?'* she thought. However, as soon as she had missed, the team applauded anyway and Alex made way for the next taker. A few mutters of 'never mind, Alex', 'you will get there' could be heard but that didn't ease the disappointment Alex felt.

On the drive home, Alex had asked her dad if he could help her practice in the park. She wasn't going to stop until she felt better about this penalty. They pulled over and headed to the goal post with the ball from the boot of the car. 'Once I score 20, then we can leave,' Alex said.She wasn't sure if it was the lack of pressure on her knowing that her teammates weren't all watching, or that her dad wasn't as quick as he used to be, but the 20 scored penalties came from 25 attempts. Alex wasn't feeling 100% better about the miss in training but spending time playing football with her dad reminded her of her love for both the game and the support she had from her family. They would do anything to help her achieve her dream.

The next assembly started as normal until she noticed a presentation on the screen, looking at the picture on the screen she knew instantly – that was Wembley. Alex had watched enough FA cup finals to know Wembley when she saw it. The head teacher began by asking the pupils if anyone knew where this was – instantly Alex shouted up with the answer. They all began to wonder why the assembly was not talking about the usual issues with the queues for lunches or the level of graffiti in the toilets, but about something interesting for a change. As part of their scheme for keeping kids playing sport, The FA had arranged a match where selected schools from around the UK could compete for a chance to play at Wembley. Alex's eyes lit up, she could barely sit still in her chair as she was desperate to know more. Two lucky schools would be selected from the many that applied to take their families down to Wembley for the 'school youth cup'. To make this opportunity even better, they were told that there might be a few scouts and professionals there to see. This was what Alex had always dreamed of,watching the England Lionesses become

European champions was one of the best moments of her life so far. Her ambition was to one day be in the shoes of Leah Williamson and captain her team to glory at Wembley.

That evening, she went home and spend most of the night day dreaming whilst looking at her Beth Mead poster. Could she be so lucky to get a chance to play at Wembley? Could she be like Ellen White, Ella Toone and Millie Bright and win a trophy at one of the most famous stadiums in the world? The wait for the result was almost too much to bear. The next week was a blur. Every spare moment was spent practicing in the park or thinking watching videos of previous matches there, trying to imagine what it may feel like to walk onto that pitch. The school had explained that there was going to be a live draw where balls are drawn to decide which schools were going to be picked to play the match at Wembley.

The assembly finally arrived, each school was going to live stream the draw. The teams were going to be selected through a draw the same as they do for the champions league, the world cup and many other competitions. As there were so many schools that entered, they had to do it in a number of different rounds. The first round was selecting the two regions where the schools were located, then this was when the individual schools were picked. The balls were given a number. This number matched up to a region, as the balls were put into what looked like a giant fishbowl, the whole assembly hall held their breath. England legend Jill Scott was responsible for picking the balls out of the bowls. After she wished everyone luck, she picked out the first ball – number 26.There were a couple of seconds when the school were trying to remember which region was number 26 –finally it was announced as the west midlands. This announcement was met with a lot of groans from the assembly hall as they know they have one more chance before they can even have their school put into the bowl. The list of regions were flashed up onto the screen. Billy in the front row stood up and said that's us, North East is number 8! It was then time for Jill to reach into the bowl for the region that will play a school from the West Midlands at Wembley. The ball was pulled out and number 8 was announced! The assembly cheered and then were quickly reminded that this was not to say that they will be the school selected from the North East.

The next set of balls were brought over in a bag to be dropped into the second bowl. This was full of the individual schools from the West Midlands. The ball was selected and this time number 52 was announced as the first lucky school to be on their way to Wembley was St Peters Academy. Alex could only imagine the elation that they would have been the feeling of knowing that they were going to be living her dream. Alex knew there was very little chance of Bluedale High being selected but she couldn't let herself think of how she would feel if they weren't picked. The final set of balls were brought out and put into the final bowl and as Jill reached her hand in to pick out the last ball Alex shut her eyes, she just couldn't look. The next moment she knew was the whole school erupting in cheers then she looked at the screen, on the screen was the match fixture for Wembley. St Peters Academy VS Bluedale High School. Alex couldn't take her eyes off the screen, thinking at any minute they would announce that they had made a mistake, this was too good to be true.

There wasn't much time to gather their thoughts, as soon as the announcement was finished then the head teacher told everyone to make their way to their first lessons as this had overlapped into first period. They were going to all be sent an email as to what was going to happen. The school was going to try to get as many people to the game as they could to support the school. There wasn't much else going on other than talking about Wembley, even the people who weren't on the football team seemed to realise the enormousness of the opportunity that they had. There were already whispers about who would be at the game, almost every player Alex had ever heard of got a mention at some point. The excitement was impossible to measure.

As the match was quickly approaching, the school team arranged for there to be a practice most nights. They worked on all areas of the game and talked thorough every tactic imaginable. Alex was enjoying playing with a team so often and she couldn't get enough of the advice that was given and the fun she was having with her squad. They all felt like they had developed a bond being around each other so much, all working towards one goal, the 90 minutes at Wembley.

Soon it was time to head down. In the school's email, they asked for as many local bus companies to help where they can to take as many people from the school. The FA said that they can have as many tickets as they needed for friends and family, with the remaining tickets split between the other schools that applied but didn't get chosen. The team from Bluedale drove down on a coach the night before so they could be rested for the next day, then the families followed down to be taken directly to Wembley. Alex had been to London once before in the school holidays with her mum, dad and George but this time felt different. This wasn't just a trip away, it could be the start of something special if the rumours were true about who was going to be watching.

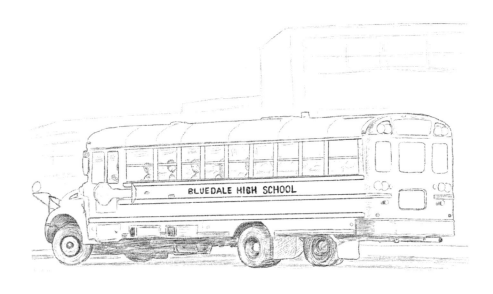

On the morning of the game, the team woke up and all gathered in the hotel reception for a schedule of the day. They were to have breakfast and then get the tube to Wembley so they can have the morning there to prepare before the kick off at 2pm. Alex felt too nervous to eat but knew she had to if she was going to have enough energy to play a game of football later. She had porridge and a banana. The coaches asked the hotel if they could take more bananas for the team for throughout the morning incase anyone needed more energy. The team packed up their bags and then off to Wembley!

Once at the stadium, they were amazed by how huge it was. This 90,000-seater stadium was even more incredible than she had imagined; walking up Wembley way was definitely something that Alex can tick off her bucket list. The FA had arranged for the teams to walk out onto the pitch before the game so they can see inside before kick-off. The first thing Alex noticed about the pitch was the sign on the railings 'where players enter and legends leave'. Alex had to pinch herself that she was actually there. Then once she looked away from the sign, she was taken aback by the number of seats in the stadium; it was overwhelming. *'How can they ever fill this many seats?'* she thought. She knew that there would not be a full crowd today but any crowd would be the bigger than the spectators that sometimes turned up to watch their five a side games at the park. Alex felt like she was on a stadium tour and kept forgetting that in a few hours her team will be playing on this pitch.

Alex was desperately beginning to hope that she had made the starting line-up. Both teams were organised onto the pitch at the half way line for a photo. This was when she noticed a couple of figures walking over from the tunnel. As they walked closer, people began to mutter. 'That's them,' she heard. 'I'm serious it is.' Alex stared at the figures until she could make one of them out. 'It's Harry Kane,' everyone instantly lost their cool and began to shout his name. The second figure came closer and then another wave of excitement filled the teams. 'It's Leah Williamson'. *No way!* Alex thought. The England captains were walking towards her and she had no idea how to react, and she could not wipe the smile from her face. Harry and Leah stood in front of both of the teams and then there were a number of photos taken. After the photos, Alex thought that they would both just leave and then carry on with their day, but they didn't; they both took turns to speak to both of the teams and help calm their nerves. As Leah walked around the group, she came to Alex, 'you're such an inspiration, and I want to be just like you one day,' Alex said. Leah smiled and said that she could be, and she was once a girl like Alex with a dream to play football for England. That moment there was by far the best moment of Alex's life, getting the opportunity to talk to one of her heroes was something that she never thought would happen. Harry and Leah then said the teams needed to go in to start to get changed before the crowds began to take their seats, they also said that they would be watching!

The teams were led down into the dressing rooms and they began to get changed for their match. Each player was talking about how amazing it was for the England captains to have the time to talk to them and how they all wanted to be like them one day. Everyone in the dressing room had the same dream, and today could be the start of fulfilling that dream too. The coaches all came into the room to go through the starting line-up. This was when Alex would find out if she was even going to play. As the listed the players from goal keeper through defence and midfield, they finally got to striker, Alex was starting upfront! The coaches then went through the subs bench and said that they were going to try to get as many people the opportunity to play as possible,but they will need to judge how the game is going for who they would bring off. Alex was thrilled but they didn't have much time to get too excited as they needed to head out for their warm up. By this time the crowds were

beginning to trickle in, as more and more people started to fill their seats then things became more real, this was actually happening.

The teams finished their warm up and then this was it, the final piece of preparation before they head out for real, no more warm ups, no more taking in the surroundings, this was now time to shine. As the teams were walked to the tunnel the players all had a moment of realisation that this was Wembley and not many people get to stand where they are and do what they are just about to do. The crowd were cheering and the teams walked out. Alex knew that her family were there but trying to look for them in the stands was pointless and there was just a sea of people with arms and flags waving. Both teams gathered for a team photo and than took their positions on the pitch for kick-off. Things were abit frantic in the first five minutes as both teams had the adrenaline hit that came with the occasion, but then they started to string a few passes together and settle as a team. James got the ball around the half way line and Alex started to make her run, staying slightly behind the defender to stay onside. James played the ball over the defender and Alex was through on goal with just the keeper to beat. Alex struck the ball with the inside of her right foot and somehow the keeper managed to stick out a leg and just deflect it away for a corner. The crowd gasped then clapped as the game was beginning to open up. The team had a corner and took it quickly but lost possession and St Peters were away up with wing with most of our players still around the box. The defenders quickly ran and tried to get back but their striker was so fast they slotted the ball into the bottom right hand corner and they were 1–0 up. Alex knew that they needed to regroup quickly to not let themselves get too affected by the goal and try to get one themselves. There were a few more chances in the game but nothing too much trouble for the goal keepers. Then before they knew it, the half time whistle went.

At half time, the players were all told by their coaches that they were doing a great job and then a 1–0 lead is not game over. They made a couple of changes and then back out to warm up before the other team gets onto the pitch. The fans all cheered again when the players came back out, this gave them motivation to push on and try to get an early goal second half. About 15 minutes into the second half Bluedale received a yellow card for an over aggressive tackle just outside of their box. As St Peters went to take their free kick, Alex knew that she was fast and if she was to get the ball from this then she could take the ball high up the pitch to help the team. The free kick was stopped at the wall and then Sophie passed it up to Alex. 'Run,' shouted her teammates. Alex sprinted with the ball but then realised that there was a defender between her and the goal, she chipped the ball passed them but was brought down by the defenders foot as she tried to run passed. Bluedale had trained for a free-kick in this position, they were either going to go for goal or pass it across the outside of the box for Alex to run onto. The arm signal let the players know that the second option was the plan. Alex knew that she needed to get away from her marker quickly so they could pass it into a good position for her to shoot from. The whistle went and Alex spun her marker and sprinted towards the outside of the box, by this time the ball had been travelling to meet her, Alex had gone through this so many times she did not even need to look at where the goal was, she put her head down and her laces though the ball, then she held her breath. The ball travelled for what seemed like forever but then flew passed the keepers outstretched gloves and into the top corner. The stadium erupted and Alex ran down the wing to the coaches. They all celebrated together and watched as the other team all questioned how they let that happen.

Alex could tell by the crowd's reactions that the game was almost over.If it stayed as a draw, then it would go to penalties. They were told before the game that they wouldn't need to play extra time as 90 minutes for school teams is already a long time. The coaches made some last minute substitutions for the players that will be needed to take penalties. Alex assumed that she would be one of the ones that were taken off as she missed her penalty in her first training session and her confidence never fully returned, but the final whistle went and she was still on the pitch. The teams were allowed a five minute break to have drinks, stretch and go over the order of who will be taking the penalties and when.

In these five minutes, Alex asked if they forgot to take her off and they said no, 'You have had a fantastic game and you deserve to be able to take the last penalty'. Alex knew that taking the last penalty is for people who often are responsible for the team winning or losing – she felt her legs go to jelly. The coaches went through the order and had a separate chat with the goalkeeper to try to get them prepared for the shots that were going to come their way.

The stadium went silent as the players walked over to the goal and the first player positioned the ball on the penalty spot to take the first kick. Bluedale were kicking second so St Peters were up first. First player took a long run up and straight down the middle – goal! The crowd all cheered and the player celebrated quickly before returning to stand with their teammates who were left to kick. The next couple for each team were standard top corner penalties where the keeper has no chance of saving. The score was 3–3 and it was St Peters turn to shoot next. The player took a small run, paused and then ran again then kicked the ball. 'It's over the bar,' said James. They had missed their fourth penalty. Bluedale knew that it was in their hand now, if they score the next two then they win. James was the second last person to take their penalty for Bluedale. He was confident and placed the ball calmly on the spot, with a short run up it was in the back of the net. Just one chance for St Peters otherwise Bluedale win. Their final player got the ball and stood over it staring at the goal for about 30 seconds before placing it and walking back for his run up. Alex knew that if they score this then it was all down to her. St Peters calmly slotted their last penalty to the left of the Bluedale keeper to make it level again. Alex felt the eyes of the entire stadium on her as she walked up for that last penalty. She began to run through all of the preparation she had done since her first training session miss. Alex, like all the players before her, walked up to the spot and placed the ball down. The referee reminded the goalkeeper to stay on their line and for Alex to wait for the whistle, they both nodded. Then the whistle went, Alex's head was clear and all she could remember was the sign written before the pitch at the start of the day 'where players enter and legends leave' – this was her time to be a legend. She took a few steps back, a deep breath and then went for it. The ball flew off Alex's foot and smashed into the bottom corner, she had done it! She turned around as her teammates were all already half way down the pitch to congratulate her, she's not sure how it happened but she ended up being lifted up into the air by her team and all she could hear was the crowd clapping and cheering. The celebrations seemed to go on for ages as the team did a lap of the pitch to applaud everyone who came to see them. As they were walking round she saw her dad, mum and brother George, all of them had tears in their eyes knowing how important this moment was to Alex.

The players all shook hands with the opposite teams as the stands were being wheeled out for the trophy lift. To Alex this didn't seem real. This only happened to people on the TV and not to her. Once the stand was ready, St Peters all lined up to receive their medals and were greeted with a big cheer from the crowd. Then finally it was the time for Bluedale to collect their prize. One by one they were presented with their medals and made their way onto the podium so they could claim their trophy. The atmosphere was electric and the noise was like nothing Alex had ever heard before. A moment of realisation had set in and Alex had begun to realise that, as a team, they had just done. The sound of Sweet Caroline rang out through the stadium and then the team all gathered for the trophy lift! As it was lifted then the noise somehow got louder. Each player had a chance to lift the trophy and each time the crowd cheered, every player had that special memory to keep forever. Once the crowds had started to leave, the players were able finally make their way down the tunnel to meet up with their family and friends. Alex's dad ran up to her and gave her a huge hug!

'I'm so proud of you, kid,' he said, 'you have followed your dream and look at what you can achieve'. The family talked for hours about the game and all the times they cheered when Alex was on the ball. Alex had never seen them so proud and it gave her a sense of self believe she had never had before.

Just before the teams were going to pack up and leave, the coaches from Bluedale came in and asked to speak to Alex and James. Fearing the worst, they both left the changing rooms slowly and walked over to where they were. They were standing with a man and a woman and they both looked important. They were both desperately trying to think of what they could be saying to them, what had they done wrong. The coaches then introduced Alex and James to them. They were scouts from Arsenal academy! They explained how they were impressed by them both and how they wanted to know if they were interested in a trial for the girls and boys academy. Alex didn't know what to say. She watched Beth Mead, Leah Williamson and Vivianne Miedema play for Arsenal Women week in, week out and to be able to have the opportunity to maybe represent the same team as them was unbelievable. Both Alex and James said yes and their parents later joined the conversation. They later found out that their parents already knew but wanted this to be a surprise for them. Everyone was so excited that they have an opportunity to impress at Arsenal. The scouts said for them to finish the school year and they made arrangements for them to travel down in the summer holidays to have a trial. Until then they had to keep working hard and get through the first lot of practice exams! Alex and James had done it, proven to themselves that with hard work and determination that even the most impossible dream can come true. The self-belief that this tournament had given every member of the team reflected on their moods back at school.

The team returned back to school as heroes and were given a celebration assembly where they all wore their medals and lifted the trophy again. Each time they got their hands on that trophy the feeling got better and better, they were champions. The school team continued to train and look forward to anytime they can play a competitive match. As the school term came to an end the pupils were all looking forward to what holidays they were going on or what they were going to be doing for the next six weeks. Alex had thought about nothing but the Arsenal academy trials since they had had the conversation with the scouts. On the first day of the holidays, the family packed up the car and made the long drive down to London to the Arsenal academy. Standing outside of the doors before they went in, Alex's dad took her to one side for one last pep talk before she was due to start the biggest training session of her life. 'Believe in yourself, kid.' Andshe always did.